A Visit From the Tooth Fairy

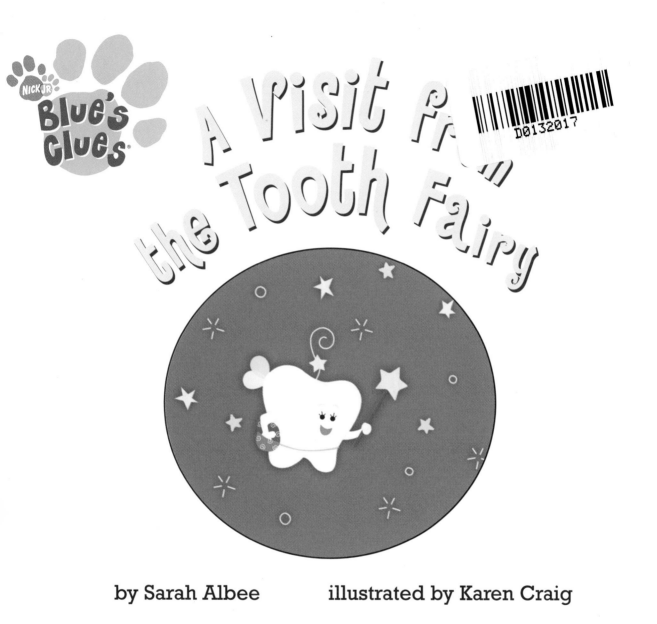

by Sarah Albee   illustrated by Karen Craig

Simon Spotlight/Nick Jr.

New York   London   Toronto   Sydney   Singapore

Based on the TV series *Blue's Clues*® created by Traci Paige Johnson,
Todd Kessler, and Angela C. Santomero as seen on Nick Jr.®
On *Blue's Clues*, Joe is played by Donovan Patton. Photos by Joan Marcus.

SIMON SPOTLIGHT
An imprint of Simon & Schuster Children's Publishing Division
1230 Avenue of the Americas, New York, New York 10020
Copyright © 2004 Viacom International Inc.
All rights reserved. NICKELODEON, NICK JR., *Blue's Clues*, and all related titles, logos,
and characters are trademarks of Viacom International Inc.
All rights reserved, including the right of reproduction in whole or in part in any form.
SIMON SPOTLIGHT and colophon are registered trademarks of Simon & Schuster.
Manufactured in the United States of America
First Edition   10 9 8 7 6 5 4 3 2 1
ISBN 0-689-86271-7

One morning, while Blue was brushing her teeth, she suddenly noticed a funny feeling in her mouth. One of her teeth was moving a little! She wiggled it back and forth, slowly at first, and then a bit faster.

"I have a loose tooth!" she said excitedly. Then she dashed off to find Joe.

"Wow, you have a loose tooth?" asked Joe in amazement. "Why is it loose?"

"Blue's tooth is ready to come out," explained Mrs. Pepper.

"What will you do with your tooth after it comes out?" Joe wondered.

"I'll put it under my pillow," said Blue, "so the Tooth Fairy can come!"

At school that day Blue proudly showed her loose tooth to Miss Marigold. Then she showed her friends.

"Does it hurt?" asked Periwinkle.

"Not a bit," Blue replied.

"Will it hurt when it comes out?" asked Magenta.

Blue looked a little worried. "I don't think so," she said.

"I guess we'll have to wait and see."

"Have you ever seen the Tooth Fairy?" asked Green Puppy.

"No," Blue replied. "I wonder what she looks like."

"Why don't we draw some pictures of what we think the Tooth Fairy looks like?" Miss Marigold suggested. So that's what the class did.

Every day Blue's tooth got a little looser.

She wiggled it while she read.

She wiggled it while she played.

She even wiggled it
while she took a bath.

After a few more days Blue's tooth became so loose she could wiggle it with her tongue.

And then during Music Time, it happened! Blue was wiggle-wiggle-wiggling her tooth when suddenly . . . it fell out! And it didn't hurt a bit!

Miss Marigold put Blue's tooth in a special box so Blue could keep it safe.

Blue proudly showed her friends the tooth. She showed them the space where the tooth used to be. It was fun to feel the empty place with her tongue.

"Soon a grown-up tooth will begin to grow in the space where you lost your baby tooth," said Miss Marigold.

"This is so exciting!" said Joe when he saw Blue's tooth. "Do you think the Tooth Fairy will really come tonight?"

"I hope so," said Blue. "But Miss Marigold says no one knows what she looks like, because she only comes if you're asleep."

Before she went to bed that night Blue put her tooth under her pillow.

That night Blue had a dream. She dreamed the Tooth Fairy came to visit her.

"Hello, Blue," said the Tooth Fairy. "What a big girl you are to have lost a tooth!"

Blue smiled to show the Tooth Fairy the space where her tooth had been.

The Tooth Fairy reached under Blue's pillow and pulled out the tooth. "Well!" she said delightedly. "This is a very lovely tooth!"

"Thanks!" said Blue.

"I will take good care of it," said the Tooth Fairy as she carefully placed the tooth in her special pouch. Then she waved her wand and disappeared in a cloud of sparkly dust.

When Blue woke up the next morning the first thing she did was feel under her pillow.

"The Tooth Fairy came! The Tooth Fairy came!" she shouted. "She took my tooth and left me a surprise!"

Blue dashed away to tell Joe.

Joe was just as excited as Blue. "You were right, Blue! The Tooth Fairy really did come!" he said.

Blue just smiled a great, big smile.